D1245958

THE YOUNG FEDERALISTS

"Abigail Readlinger has given us a marvelous tale of a time-traveling band of children—offspring of an American history buff—who find themselves discussing the nature of government over tea with none other than Alexander Hamilton! They meet the founding father and his family, just as he is constructing the case he wishes to make to his fellow citizens of New York to persuade them to ratify the Constitution he and his allies drafted during their convention in Philadelphia. Everyone learns!"

—Robert P. George, McCormick Professor of Jurisprudence, Princeton University

"Abby Readlinger has written a charming story about a magical encounter with Alexander Hamilton, connecting our country's founding principles to the everyday lives of children (and their parents). *The Young Federalists* will introduce young readers to the blessings of our 'union under one government,' as Hamilton himself put it."

—Greg Grimsal, New Orleans attorney

"Who says history and civics are boring, incomprehensible disciplines? Certainly not readers who have traveled with the Kennedy children to meet Alexander Hamilton and understand how Federalist Paper No. 1 affects them today. Fantasy, philosophy, adventure, and friendship combine in Readlinger's short book and leave us craving another installment of the Kennedy family adventures."

—Dr. Karen Ristuccia, Former Academic Dean

"Abby Readlinger has done the world a tremendous favor: She's made a collection of critical founding documents accessible and interesting to the next generation by turning it into a time travel adventure. *The Federalist Papers* have been too long ignored by modern school curriculums, which our founding generation surely would not have understood. James Madison described the papers as 'the most authentic exposition of the text of the federal Constitution,' while Thomas Jefferson considered it one of the 'best guides' for understanding the 'distinctive principles . . . of the United States.' Readlinger's creative take on the subject humanizes the Founders— and America's foundational principles. Her book is sorely needed in these trying times."

—Tara Ross, author of *Why We Need the Electoral College* and *She Fought, Too: Stories of Revolutionary War Heroes*

"As a media professional who greatly appreciates and respects the ability to distill complex ideas and writing into relatable communication, I find this book to be refreshing, entertaining, and informative, all at once. As a mother of two, who wants to instill in her young children the love of history and reading, I highly recommend *The Young Federalists* to readers of all ages who want to be entertained and challenged to learn at the same time."

—Tara Maitra, Chief Commercial Officer, BBC Studios Americas

THE YOUNG FEDERALISTS

MASCOT KIDS!

an imprint of Amplify Publishing Group

www.mascotbooks.com

The Young Federalists

For more information, please contact:
Mascot Kids, an imprint of Amplify Publishing Group
620 Herndon Parkway, Suite 320
Herndon, VA 20170
info@mascotbooks.com

Library of Congress Control Number: 2022903918

CPSIA Code: PRV0622A

ISBN-13: 978-1-63755-171-4

Printed in the United States

For HL9:
We all thought Hamilton was the hardest to comprehend.
Hopefully, this makes his in-depth writing enjoyable
for younger audiences.

NOTE TO READERS

Think about everything you've done today.

Maybe you've crossed the street. Maybe you went to your local café for the new seasonal pastry. Or maybe you've just picked up a children's book on *The Federalist Papers*.

Something is the same in every case. Every action you've taken, every step you've made, is the result of something or someone abiding by the processes of the law. You crossed the road safely because there's a law prohibiting cars from driving through red lights. You bought your pastry for an additional cost because of laws on sales tax. The book you are holding is the result of a publishing company printing according to the laws of the press.

So we're surrounded by laws.

But what put those laws into action?

The Constitution of the United States: a document written over two centuries ago that provides the basic framework for every law in our nation.

But what are the reasons behind why we have this "Constitution" and its laws?

That . . . is a good question.

And it's one that is answered by a very important series of eighty-five documents called *The Federalist Papers* written by Alexander Hamilton, John Jay, and James Madison.

This book—*The Young Federalists*—wants to give you the opportunity to find the answers.

Why does America have the Constitution? What made it important then? What makes it important now? What will make it important for the future?

Remember, everything you do, all the freedoms you enjoy, are the result of our nation's great Constitution. Don't you think we should long to know and understand all that we can about what went into making America a truly amazing country?

If you're ready to learn, if you're ready to stand up for your freedoms, if you're ready to . . .

Oh, go on!

Flip the page and read on!

Sincerely,

Abby Readlinger

NOTE TO PARENTS

There has never been a more earnest advocate for encouraging others to read *The Federalist Papers* than Justice Antonin Scalia. During one of his many lectures, he urged the audience to "get a copy of *The Federalist Papers*, read it, underline it, and dog-ear it." I have to admit, I've taken those words to heart. My own copy of *The Federalist Papers* sits next to me as I write, covered in ink and highlighter, bended, folded, and annotated.

Why?

Because, although written over two centuries ago, *The Federalist Papers* still hold profound value in understanding and preserving the United States of America. The Constitution is the founding document of our great nation, and through it, we receive the rights, freedoms, and privileges of Americans. But what are the reasons behind the Constitution? How and why did America constitute a completely revolutionary system of government? The answers are found in the words of Alexander Hamilton, John Jay, and James Madison: authors of all eight-five Federalist Papers.

And yet, though so clearly crucial, *The Federalist Papers* are almost only read by those in law school or working in government. The benefits of the Constitution apply to all Americans, and because of this, every American should not only understand, but long to understand the origin and reasons behind the nature of their freedoms.

Without perceiving and studying the reasons behind our freedoms, we begin to take them for granted. Once they are taken for granted, we seem to forget their importance. And when we forget their importance, they are quickly and easily taken away.

In writing *The Young Federalists*, I have taken a step I believe is much needed in America. I am writing to encourage the younger generation—your children and grandchildren—to read the fundamental documents behind the Constitution. I am writing for the sake of all those who enjoy America's benefits, so that they might see and understand the reasons behind their rights. I am writing in the belief that our freedoms should never be taken for granted. I am writing with joy, in the great hope that every American will take up their copy of *The Federalist Papers*, read it, underline it, and dog-ear it to their heart's content.

Sincerely,
Abby Readlinger

CHAPTER ONE

"MAYBE WE SHOULD JUST POSTPONE THE meeting to another day?" Andrew Jackson Kennedy, or AJ, as he liked to be called, suggested to the four, ten-year-old boys sitting around him on the playground. They had been trying unsuccessfully for the last hour to put up a new **government** in their club.

"Yeah, I agree with AJ. We can't come up with anything that we all agree on!" said Tyler, a tall, skinny boy with glasses.

"Why do we even have to change it?" asked another boy, Jimmy.

"We already went over it, Jimmy! Mikey joined our club, so now we have to find a position for him! It isn't fair for him to just be a citizen when I'm the president, Tyler is the Supreme Court, and you and Cole are the House of Representatives and the Senate!" AJ told his friend.

"Yep! That's why I think we should have **elections!** If we all **vote** on the positions again, Mikey will have a fair chance of getting one!" exclaimed Cole, a short boy with a loud voice.

"The only problem with that is, there will be one person without a job!" AJ reasoned for what seemed to be the hundredth time.

All the boys were quiet. They loved being part of the club, and none of them wanted to feel left out. Then, suddenly, Mikey Brown spoke up.

"Hey, AJ," he said. "Maybe your dad knows another position that we could add to the club. Then everyone would have a position!"

"You're right!" AJ said. AJ's dad was what the government called the **Archivist of the United States**, which meant that he took care of all the important documents at the **National Archives**, like the **Bill of Rights**, the **Constitution**, and the **Declaration of Independence**. AJ was sure that no one in the world loved American history as much as his father. Dad would be the perfect person to give them an idea for the fifth position.

"Yeah! That's a great idea, Mikey!" Tyler agreed. "AJ, when your dad comes to pick you up, we can ask him!"

"Perfect!" AJ said as he jumped off the playground and onto the wood chips below. He scratched his head. "All right, what game should we play today?" As president, AJ could choose which game the club would play and the rest of the boys would either agree or disagree.

"Freeze tag?" he offered. "All in favor, say 'aye.'"

Cole, Mikey, Jimmy, and Tyler cheered "aye" in response.

After springing from their sitting positions, the boys selected the "it" and began sprinting all around the fields. AJ, who was chosen as the tagger, dashed after his friends. He was almost about to grab Jimmy when something out of the corner of his eye caught his attention: something shiny. He stopped short of grabbing Jimmy and jogged to where the light had caught his eye.

"Hey, guys!" he called. "Look, I think I found something!"

"No way, we aren't falling for that one!" Cole said, as his small head poked out from behind a nearby tree.

"No, really!" AJ said as he bent down to pick up the shiny case about the size of a wallet.

The four boys finally relented and walked to where AJ was standing.

"I wonder what it is?" AJ said as he examined the object.

"Open it!" The boys chanted in a chorus. Giving in, AJ pressed a black button on the wallet, and it clicked open.

The boys gasped.

Inside the wallet were ten, green ten-dollar bills.

CHAPTER TWO

"WOW!" AJ BREATHED AS HE FELT THE money between his fingers. Cole stood on his tiptoes and looked down at AJ's hands.

"One hundred dollars! We're rich!" he shouted as he reached for the money.

AJ pulled it back from Cole. "Hold on. Someone may have lost this. We need to wait and see."

"No way!" Jimmy said as he lunged for the wallet. "It's got dirt all over it. I bet it's been there for a long time!"

"No, Jimmy." AJ put his hand up and stopped the boys from grabbing the wallet.

"You just want to keep it for yourself!" Tyler cried, angry at AJ for stopping him.

AJ felt annoyed. "Well, it was *me* who found it! If we can't find the owner, then it should be mine!"

"You wouldn't have seen it if you hadn't been chasing me!" Jimmy said.

"Yeah, and if I hadn't chosen you to be 'it,' then I could have found it!" Mikey agreed.

"But I did find it . . . I guess I could split some of the bills and you guys could each have five dollars, and I could keep the rest?" AJ suggested, wanting to make his friends happy.

Cole shook his head. "You think you have top priority because you're the president! Well, guess what, Andrew Jackson—when we have elections, you won't have my vote!"

"Hey! That's not fair! I'm not doing it because I'm the president; I'm doing it because I found it!"

"Cole's right, AJ!" Jimmy sneered. "You're corrupting your power!"

"I am not!"

The boys broke out into a series of arguments until a tall, skinny man wearing a blue suit and a shiny American flag lapel pin stopped the fight.

"Hey! What's going on here, boys?" the man asked.

AJ looked at the face of Mr. Kennedy, his father. Dad had red hair like his son and a large, toothy grin that showed two rows of perfect, shining teeth which could make anyone feel better. At the sight of AJ's father, all three boys stopped their talking and sat tight; they were ready to listen to the wise words of the American history scholar.

"Well?" Dad asked.

AJ spoke up. "Well, Dad, I found some money by the tree, and . . . If we don't find the owner, we were just trying to figure out how we were gonna split it."

"Ah, I see." Dad looked at the boys thoughtfully. "Well, how about this: I'll look around for the owner, and if I don't find them in a week, then—and only then—will I help you decide what to do with the money. That sound fair?" The tone in his voice implied that the decision was, in fact, a very fair one.

"Yes, Mr. Kennedy," the boys mumbled.

Dad smiled at them with his big, toothy grin. "Don't look glum, boys. Listen, you're a group of remarkable young men with strong friendships; don't let that bond be broken by a little squabble. Every government has its problems. They just need to go back to the root of why they started that government, and there they will find the answer to their problem. I know you men can figure it out." He gave them a curt nod and reached for the wallet in AJ's hand. "I'll hold onto this and see if anyone around here has lost a wallet. All right?"

The boys nodded. They knew that even though Mr. Kennedy was AJ's dad, he would be just as fair as any other person on the matter.

"Sorry, AJ," Jimmy and Cole said when Dad stopped speaking.

"That's okay," AJ said. "Friends?"

"Friends," they echoed.

CHAPTER THREE

"DAD?" AJ SAID AS HE AND HIS FATHER
walked back to the car. "I just have a feeling that our government isn't working."

His father nodded understandingly. "But you're back to being friends?"

"Oh, yes!" AJ assured him. "We'll always be friends, but when there's a problem, we can never figure out a way to settle it. Everyone always has their own ideas, even me! We just can't figure out what's best. I'm wondering whether having a government is a good idea. If we can't agree, what's the use in having one?"

Mr. Kennedy laughed and stuck his hands deep in his pockets. "You're a smart boy, AJ. Clever, determined—one of the reasons why the name Andrew Jackson fits you so well!"

AJ smiled. Dad had named each of his five children in honor of one of his favorite leaders: AJ was named after the courageous **General Andrew Jackson**; Reagan, his thirteen-year-old sister, was named after **President Ronald Reagan**; and Dolley, his seven-year-old sister, was named after **First Lady Dolley Madison**, the wife of **President**

James Madison. Then there were the four-year-old twins, Theo and Abe, named after **President Theodore Roosevelt** and **President Abraham Lincoln**.

"So, Dad?" AJ asked again. "What should we do with our club?"

Dad didn't answer. He just looked ahead with a funny expression, as if he knew something that AJ didn't.

"What?" AJ asked, curious.

"Oh, nothing," Dad laughed, keeping his eyes straight ahead.

AJ raised his eyebrows but didn't say anything and hopped into the car with his father. Dolley and Reagan were already in the car.

"What are you guys doing here?" he asked.

Reagan folded her arms and shrugged her shoulders. "We just came back from the debate tournament. Dad said he would take us to the café in the Archives while he grabbed some paperwork."

"Actually, I got my paperwork already, but I think we'll stop in the **Rotunda** at the Archives for a little bit and look at some of the documents. You guys haven't been there yet, right?"

Dolley giggled. "Daddy! We've been there a million times."

"Oh, really?" Dad looked as if it were all he could do to keep from laughing.

"Dad, what are you talking about?" Reagan asked.

"Oh, nothing at all. Just . . ."

"What?" All three of the kids shouted in curiosity.

"I think that you should have one more look at those documents. AJ, they might help you find what you're looking for to help you solve your club's government problems."

"Dad? Why are you smiling so weird?" Dolley asked.

That just made Dad smile even more. "No reason."

AJ turned to his sisters, and they all shared a look of confusion, doubt, and maybe even a little bit of excitement. Then, in unison, they all shrugged as Mr. Kennedy headed his car in the direction of the **National Archives Museum.**

CHAPTER FOUR

"MR. KENNEDY! MR. KENNEDY! THANK
goodness you came in time; the president is on the phone!" A
young man in a black suit came charging down the central stairs
of the National Archives Museum as AJ, Reagan, Dolley, and Dad
walked into the building.

"Yes, Jameson. I know. I'll be there in a minute." Dad nodded
toward the young man, motioning with his hands for him to
calm down. "The president scheduled this meeting with me, and
it doesn't start for another three-and-a-half minutes."

The young man didn't look any calmer. "Oh, uh—yes, sir. I was
just nervous . . . will you come now?" he asked frantically.

"Yes, I'll come. I just want to ask Tom to keep an eye on the kids
while I have the meeting."

"I can do that!" Mr. Jameson said.

Dad looked at his children and smiled. "No, I think I'd rather
do it myself."

Mr. Jameson, clearly defeated, nodded and walked back up the steps.

The Kennedy children looked around at each other in wonder. Why would their dad have brought them to the Archives if he knew he had a meeting? And why would he leave them in the care of Tom, one of the custodians?

"Well, c'mon. Don't just stand there! Let's go into history!" Dad shouted as they walked into the Rotunda. *Let's go into history!* was his favorite phrase whenever he was about to read, recite, or show his children an amazing part of the American government.

"Dad, why did you bring us here if you knew that you had a meeting?" Reagan asked as she shook her head in confusion.

Mr. Kennedy smiled and kept walking along the Rotunda, eyeing the documents with admiration.

"Dad?" Reagan asked again. "Dad . . . ? Dad!"

"Remember that phrase, kid: Let's go into history!" he murmured to himself and then turned to face his children.

"Well, I've gotta run. Mr. President is on the phone. Now, you kids know to stay with Tom, right?" Dad pointed to a tall, skinny man with large eyes and a uniform like a police officer.

The Kennedy children nodded.

"All right. *Behave*—and, uh . . . have a great time." He winked, nodded at Tom, and walked toward his office, leaving his kids with open mouths.

"Why is Daddy acting funny?" Dolley asked.

"I have no idea," Reagan said as the three of them bent over the glass case of the Declaration of Independence.

"He never acts like that . . . He's always doing proper and precise stuff. It just doesn't make sense. Why would he purposely schedule a meeting and then bring us here to do nothing?" AJ wondered. Nothing about this entire visit made sense.

Reagan nodded. "And he wouldn't answer *any* of our questions."

"Yeah, same," AJ nodded. "I was trying to ask him about my club government and he wouldn't respond. It just wasn't like him."

"Well, I guess we just sit here, then?" Dolley asked as the three of them took a seat on one of the benches. It was almost closing time for the Archives and there wasn't a single person in the room except for the three Kennedy children and Tom.

It was Tom who spoke next. "What's the matter, kids? Are these documents too old for you? Can't read the cursive?" He looked disappointed.

AJ and Dolley said, "Yes" at the same time Reagan said, "No."

Tom smiled. "Which one is it?"

"I can't read cursive," Dolley explained.

"Too old," AJ complained.

"And no to both of those," Reagan said. "I like old documents and things, but I don't see how they can answer AJ's questions about his club. He has pretty specific problems, and I don't think those papers can answer them."

Tom smiled an odd smile, just like the one Dad had given them. Then, without any warning, he started to walk out of the Rotunda.

"Hey!" Dolley cried. "My dad said that we're supposed to stay with you! Come back!"

Tom shrugged as he called back. "Well, then follow me!"

The three Kennedys looked at each other and then back at the Rotunda. In a second, they were jogging after the caretaker.

CHAPTER FIVE

"HEY, TOM! WAIT UP!" DOLLEY CALLED AS the siblings chased the janitor down a narrow stairwell and into a large storage hallway.

Tom didn't answer but kept walking faster and faster. Dolley, Reagan, and AJ would have easily caught up with him if it hadn't been for the boxes and containers that littered the halls. It seemed that they could never walk in a straight line, but Tom, on the other hand, could walk through the hallway with his eyes closed.

"Tom! We're going to lose you!" Reagan shouted.

Tom's response was to weave faster through all the boxes.

"Hurry up, Dolley!" AJ said when he turned back and saw his younger sister struggling to clamber over a large box.

"I'm trying!" she said.

"AJ, stay back with her. I'll try to catch up with Tom and see where he's leading us," Reagan commanded.

"No way! We all go together," he retorted.

"Fine," Reagan conceded. The two of them stopped for a minute and waited for little, flustered Dolley to catch up.

"Go!" Dolley called as she ran toward them. "He's going through the door!"

The three of them turned and looked toward where Tom had stopped and opened one of the biggest, oldest doors they had ever seen.

"Where are you going?" Reagan called out.

Tom smiled. "Remember that what your father said was important!" And with that, he leaped through the door and slammed it shut.

"Tom!" Dolley shouted as she ran ahead of her siblings. When her hands reached the door handle, it wouldn't budge.

"He locked it!" she realized aloud.

"What do you mean, 'He locked it'?" Reagan asked in disbelief.

"Exactly what she said. The door's locked. He must have locked us out!" AJ said, shocked. He gripped the handle with both hands but it still didn't move.

"Ugggh! You have to be kidding me!" Reagan said. She looked toward the maze of boxes and raised her eyes in a much more serious manner. "Um? Do any of you guys know how to get back to the Rotunda?"

Dolley's green eyes widened. "You mean, you don't know how to get us out of here?"

Reagan shook her head slowly. "We must have made over ten turns, and with all these boxes, it's impossible to tell where to go . . ."

"Reagan!" Dolley shrieked. "Are we lost?"

"No, no, I don't know . . . Tom *has* to come back. AJ, can't you remember anything about the . . ." Reagan broke off her sentence.

Dolley finished it. "AJ, what are you doing?"

AJ was leaning his head against the door and murmuring to himself. "I was just thinking: remember what Tom said? 'Remember what your father said was important.'"

His sisters raised their eyebrows in unison.

"What if it's like a password?" AJ blurted out, clearly excited.

Reagan raised her eyebrow skeptically.

"Oh, I get it!" Dolley cheered. "Dad told us to remember his phrase, 'Let's go into history!' Maybe if we say that, it will open the door!"

Reagan shook her head. "You guys have read too many fantasy books; there's no way that can happen."

AJ rolled his eyes. "C'mon, Dolley. Let's try. At least we are trying, instead of just sitting around like *somebody*."

"Let's go into history!" they shouted at the door.

Nothing happened.

Reagan smiled. "See?"

AJ frowned and looked at his older sister. "You have to say it with us."

"That's not going to do anything!" she insisted.

"Just *try*!" Dolley pleaded.

"Fine," Reagan said, and the three of them lined up in front of the huge door.

"Let's go into history!" they shouted.

As soon as the words left their mouths, the door seemed to burst into red, blue, and white flames that swirled together in an eerie circle. In fact, after a closer look, they weren't flames at all. They seemed to be swirling in the pattern of the American flag, but more than just the flag . . .

The Kennedy children all sucked in a breath.

To them, it looked like a portal.

A portal to history. American history.

CHAPTER SIX

"WHOA!" THE KENNEDY KIDS EXCLAIMED
in unison.

"What is it?" Dolley asked.

"I have no idea!" AJ started. "It's like a . . ."

"Portal!" Reagan said, as if she couldn't believe what was happening.

"You're the oldest!" AJ said, looking at the huge portal before them. "You go first."

Reagan was just as transfixed as he was. "No way. You think I'm walking in there? No, no, no, no, no, no . . ."

"Fine!" AJ said. "We'll do a test." He bent around to find something on the floor and came back up with an old baseball. "Okay," he said. "Here we go." He threw the ball through the colors of the American flag.

It vanished.

"Well?" AJ said. His eyes were expectant; he clearly wanted to jump in after it.

"No, AJ!" Reagan said.

"Well, we *have* to go in it. This is probably what Dad was so giddy about; he knew Tom would lead us here! They were friends when they were younger! They were probably in cahoots with . . ."

"No way."

"Yeah . . . um . . . Reagan?" AJ stopped and looked around. "Where's Dolley?"

Reagan stopped talking and looked around her. "Dolley? Dolley! Come out! I know you're hiding!"

No one answered.

"You don't think she went . . ." AJ started, his eyes wide.

Reagan nodded slowly. "I guess that means. . ."

". . .we have to go in after her," Reagan finished.

The two of them gulped. "Here goes nothing!"

They jumped in after their sister.

It felt like slimy jelly as they fell down what seemed to be an everlasting drop. Then, without any warning, the two of them landed with a thud on a hard, wooden floor.

"Dolley!" Reagan cried as she leapt to her feet and saw her little sister standing before them with a huge grin on her face.

"What took you so long?" she giggled.

"Never, ever do that again! What if this . . . ?"

AJ interrupted. "What are you *wearing*?" He pointed a finger toward the long blue dress with white lace that his younger sister was wearing.

"I have no idea!" Dolley said. She pointed at him with a grin on her face. "What are you wearing?"

AJ bent over to look at his short brown jacket, black pants, and white socks that went to his knees.

"Ahhhhh! What am I wearing?!" he screamed. "How did this happen? Where did my other clothes go . . . ?"

"Um, guys. Forget about the clothes. Where *are* we?" Reagan, in her white dress with a pink sash, threw her arms out and motioned to the room they were in. It was an attic room cluttered with old boxes, and if not for the light streaming in from the windows, Reagan would have guessed that they were still in the basement of the National Archives.

The Kennedys looked around them.

What was this place?

Where had the portal taken them?

"Reagan?" Dolley asked. "How did we get wherever we are?"

"I'm not sure, but I don't know how to get back."

"We must be in a time portal. I can't be certain, but these clothes look like late 1700s and early 1800s," AJ insisted.

"AJ, I don't know. There can't be such a thing as a time portal . . ."

"Reagan! We just went through an American flag void and came out in a completely different place—with these outfits on! Do you have another explanation?" AJ cried. His voice echoed through the attic.

"I agree with AJ!" Dolley shouted. Her voice was louder than AJ's, and Reagan tried her best to calm them both.

"Shhh. Guys, be quiet. There might be someone else . . ."

A voice was heard in the distance. "Eliza? You hear something up there? If it's those squirrels again . . ."

The voice got louder. Someone was walking up the attic steps.

CHAPTER SEVEN

"GOODNESS, ELIZA, IF IT'S THOSE SQUIR- rels again, I am going . . . well, look at that!" The Kennedy children stood still as a familiar, short man with kind, blue eyes, a large nose, and a handsome face appeared from the attic steps. He was dressed almost like AJ, except that his black jacket came a little higher up on his neck, and he wore a large, white shirt that puffed out in large bunches at the bottom of his chin. From just one look at him, the Kennedy children knew who he must be: **Alexander Hamilton**.

"And who, may I ask, are you?" Mr. Hamilton smiled and raised a playful eyebrow at the children.

"Um, sir . . . we're sorry . . . we didn't realize . . ." Reagan sputtered out, too shocked to use a full sentence.

Luckily, AJ was a fast thinker—and a good one, too. "Sorry, sir. You see, we were playing with our ball in the road, and I accidentally threw it into your open window. Not wanting to disturb you, we climbed in after it but, as you can see, certainly failed." AJ made a dramatic bow before the **Founding Father** and picked up the baseball they had thrown into the portal.

Mr. Hamilton cocked his head and laughed but didn't rebuke them for coming in. He scratched his head a little and pondered, "You know, you children must be pretty great climbers. Why, this window must be over thirty feet high!"

AJ bit his lip, but fortunately, he was saved by another person. A small woman in a dress that looked very similar to Reagan's came walking up the stairs. She had dark eyes and a kind face to match her husband's. She was equally surprised when she saw the Kennedys in her attic.

"Goodness, Alexander! Those certainly aren't squirrels!"

Mr. Hamilton laughed. "No, they certainly aren't."

The Kennedy children smiled weakly.

"Well, you children better take your ball and go. I bet your folks are expecting you."

"Oh, no, sir! We're orphans!" Dolley shouted. AJ and Reagan looked at each other and grimaced.

Luckily the white lie seemed to work. **Eliza Hamilton** clapped her hands and motioned for them to come downstairs. "Well, if you're not in a rush, then perhaps you'd like to come down and have some tea with us. **Philip, Angelica**, and little **Alex** are down there now, and they do love to be doted on by older children!"

"Eliza, these children might not want to stay . . ."

"Oh, we'd love to, sir!" Dolley said.

"That is, only for a little while," Reagan jumped in.

"Well, I'm sure Eliza would love your company . . ." Mr. Hamilton started.

"No, no, no. You'll be joining us, too, Alexander. It's about time you take a break from work and enjoy yourself."

"No, I'm afraid my work is crucial to both New York and the Constitution. I will join you for a cup of tea but then I really must keep working."

Eliza nodded her head understandingly, and the two of them

began to walk down the stairs. When she reached the bottom, she called out, "Why, don't just stand there, children. C'mon!"

The Kennedys looked at each other with mixed expressions and followed their gracious hostess down the stairs.

CHAPTER EIGHT

"SO, CHILDREN, WHAT ARE YOUR NAMES?"
Eliza asked as they walked into a large room with a sink and counter, which must have been the kitchen. Three children—two boys and a girl—were sitting peacefully on the floor with some wooden blocks.

"I'm Reagan Kennedy, this is AJ, and my sister's Dolley," Reagan said.

"I'm sorry? I didn't catch the boy's name: Ajay?" Mr. Hamilton said, confused.

"It stands for the famous General Andrew Jackson!" AJ explained.

The Hamiltons gave him blank looks. "I'm sorry to say that I've never heard of Andrew Jackson," Eliza said, handing her husband a cup of tea.

Reagan glared at AJ with a look that said, *We're in the 1780s, AJ! Andrew Jackson isn't famous yet!*

"Oh, yeah. I mean, well, he was someone our dad knew a long time ago."

The Hamiltons seemed to take that as a satisfactory answer, but just in case, Reagan changed the subject.

"Excuse me, sir," Reagan said as Mr. Hamilton mixed some sugar into his tea. "If you don't mind, what work are you doing for the Constitution?"

"So, even children like you have heard about the Constitution?" He seemed happy.

"Oh, yes, sir. We think the Constitution is a grand idea!" AJ said.

"Yes, lots of people think that, too. I'm not so sure about the state of New York, though. The Constitution was written in September, and I've been working hard ever since to gain enough popularity with the people to get them to **ratify** it. In fact, that's what I've been working on."

He sat down on a stool in the kitchen and the Kennedy children leaned in, excited.

"I'm working on something called *The Federalist Papers*. Along with a couple of my friends, **John Jay** and James Madison, I've been hoping to distribute this collection of papers in the newspapers in order to convince New Yorkers that this Constitution should be ratified."

"Hey! James Madison! I'm named after his wife!" Dolley said eagerly.

Alexander smiled. "She's a good person to be named after. Anyway, we've been working to put this collection together, and I've been chosen to write the first one. I have to lay the groundwork for all of them. I need to prove that a government can be good, and that this is the government. I need to rebuke people while also being kind, and above all, I need to prove that people—regular, ordinary, everyday people—need to make this decision."

AJ was suddenly very interested. "Are you creating the government?"

Mr. Hamilton shook his head. "No, no—I'm not creating it. The Constitution is really our government. I'm just trying to persuade people that it's the right government for them."

"What do you mean by that?" Dolley asked as she sat down on the stool next to the Founding Father.

"I think I know what he means!" answered AJ. "It's like the government I have with my friends. We can never agree on certain rules or positions, because there's always someone who thinks differently. One of us needs to prove to the others that our plan of action is the best."

"Right, AJ! It's kind of like that. You see, on July 4th, 1776, these states broke away from the mother country of England with the Declaration of Independence. When England was our government, it was a monarchy. Now, our leaders want to create a **democratic republic** with the Constitution, and in order to do so, we need states to ratify the Constitution."

"So, you need to convince the people that this is the best government for them?" Reagan asked.

"Yes." Alexander Hamilton looked down at his tea and shook his head; that was clearly where he was having trouble.

AJ spoke up. "I don't really know how to say it, but I know that government is necessary for regulation and protection, and I know you're trying to convince people that this is the best government for them, but . . ."

AJ paused to consider his next words carefully.

Mr. Hamilton nodded encouragingly.

"Is there even such a thing as a *good* government?" AJ asked.

CHAPTER NINE

ALEXANDER NODDED HIS HEAD thoughtfully. "You're a smart boy, you know that? I've been asked that question many, many times . . . but never from someone so young!" He mused over the question again. *"Is it possible that societies of men are really capable or not of establishing good government from reflection and choice, or are they forever destined to depend for their political constitutions on accident and force?"*

"I'm sorry, Mr. Hamilton?" Dolley asked, confused by his language.

"Well, it's like this, child. There have been governments in the past—many, many governments—yet all of them seem to have been derived from war or force. It's true that some of those governments may live to be the most famous of all time, but none of them derived from peace, reflection, or choice."

"Can a government be good? I mean, can people all agree on a government instead of just the strongest winning, and then establishing whatever they want?" AJ asked, thinking back to the government with his friends.

"Governments are groups of people meant to protect, and I think lots of people around the world just have the sad misconception that protection involves force, but America is different from them," he said slowly. "We're trying to establish a good government by reason and choice, which has never really been done before. I guess you could say that America—we're the test."

"So, you don't know if America is going to turn out to be a good government?" Reagan asked doubtfully.

"No one ever really knows. But this government is run by the people, based on the people's needs and values and, most importantly, their **liberty**. If we stick to the Constitution and we follow it and never breach the right of people's liberties, then we can have a good government!" Mr. Hamilton brightened. "The people need this Constitution to give them the best chance of true freedom and can be borne of reflection and choice . . . but we must never stray from that. Once we stray from the people, once we stray from the fact that every man, woman, and child is created equal, then and there our government has failed."

The Kennedy children looked in awe at the man in front of them. He was so full of courage and hope, and then they knew that they were reliving history, history that brought them their home and freedoms, and they were now here to witness it . . .

"Sir, if I may ask just one question?" Reagan asked, pulling her chair closer to the Founding Father.

"Of course; let me just grab a piece of paper. I've suddenly had some ideas."

"Well, I was wondering: If there's always a chance of liberties being taken away by the government, then why have one at all? Isn't there much less risk that way?"

Alexander Hamilton looked up. "My children, I believe that you are smarter than some adults I know, and in fact, that's another point I must add on my notes." He scribbled down on his paper and continued speaking. "I want you to imagine an island."

The children nodded.

"On that island, there is a group of thirty or so people. Think what would happen if their collective government was like the one the Constitution proposes. If they followed the exact rules, the people would generally be safe from harm. Now think of the same island, except that it was every man for himself; you would think that everyone would just go along with doing whatever they wanted, right? Well, now put human nature in the mix. Say that there is one person who wants control of everything; he's looking out for his own interests. Say he's got all of his friends, and they gang up on the rest of the people on the island and try to hurt them. Who's going to stop them? There is no government anymore; there never was one to begin with! The rest of the people are hopeless and unprotected, because they aren't united."

"I think I see," AJ said, nodding his head.

"This is my main point!" He drew a large line on the paper and spoke as he wrote the words. *"The vigor of government is essential to the security of liberty; that, in the contemplation of a sound and well-informed judgement, their interest can never be separated."*

"I get it!" Reagan said. "You're saying that while lots of people think that the government is unneeded and a huge force against their liberty, it's actually *essential* to their freedom and liberty."

"Ohh! So the people on the island with no government think that they have absolute freedom; but they don't because there's no way to secure it like a government would," AJ said.

"Exactly, my boy!" Alexander Hamilton wrote furiously on his paper.

Dolley jumped in. "So the sole job of a good government is to secure our liberties and do nothing to take them away!"

"Exactly!"

"Mr. Hamilton," Reagan said thoughtfully, "say we're back on that island with that gang who just wants to have all the power. Why would they ever agree to a government when they were clearly stronger before? I mean, they must have made up a large piece of the group on the island. If it is like that in America, the Constitution will never be ratified."

AJ shook his head. "Yeah, how can you convince the people in New York, who would be stronger without the Constitution, to ratify it?"

Alexander nodded solemnly, put his pencil down, and looked at the children.

"This is a point I know far too well. People, because we are people, always have a tendency to look where our private interests lie. It can happen in any circumstance, whether you're a child in school or an adult like me. And a fact of life is that humans look to themselves first. But the government doesn't work that way. *Happy will it be if our choice should be directed by a judicious estimate of our true interests, unperplexed and unbiased by considerations not connected with the public good.*"

"I'm not sure what you mean, sir?" Dolley asked, wrinkling her eyebrows.

"Let me think of a way to explain it. Ahh, yes, I know. Let's say there's a family, I can use mine as an example. I have three children and a wife, and it's my job to take care of them. Now let's say I had a decision to make. Take this situation: I go to work and receive a raise from my employer. What do I do with the extra money? Do I take it and buy myself a new quill pen when I already have four, or do I use that extra money to, say, fix the leak in my ceiling? The first choice would benefit me, and if I chose that road, I would be looking to my private interests. But the second would benefit everyone in the house, and I would be looking at the public interests. But note that it is *my* money; I am the one who holds the power, yet when I look at the public interests, I can see what can be done for everyone. In my paper, I want to convince everyone of the good they can do when they see more than just themselves."

"The same is true for the government, then?" AJ said. "If we want the people with lots of power to see the good of the Constitution, we can show them that it's best for everyone's interest and that if they help people, they'll be helped in the long run, too."

"Right, AJ! Because each of them will have a government to protect their liberties."

CHAPTER TEN

"ALEXANDER, ARE THE CHILDREN STILL
here? Why, it's getting dark. They should be getting home," Mrs. Hamilton called from the porch where she was sitting with her children.

"Goodness! You're right! I'm afraid I've kept them longer than I intended to, but they were just such a huge help in sketching out a plan for my first paper." He turned to the children. "I must thank you. You have no idea the help you've given me!"

"No, sir, you answered the questions. We were just here to ask them," Dolley said as she smiled sweetly.

"Yes, but the world often gets its answers from the people who ask questions. Now, you children better run along. I'm sure you've got some place to be."

The three hearts of the Kennedy children sank low. They had such a great time learning from Alexander Hamilton, and it would be hard to say goodbye. On the other hand, they couldn't wait to return home and practice all that they had been taught.

Mr. Hamilton shook their hands and motioned toward the exit. "I hope you'll come back soon." He smiled.

The Kennedys glanced nervously at each other. How could they get back to the attic?

AJ thought fast. "Oh, yes sir, but we forgot our ball in the attic. Do you mind if we go back and get it first?"

"Oh, of course." Mr. Hamilton winked. "After all, you have to get back to where you came from."

The children's mouths gaped open.

"What?" Reagan said. "You—you . . . you know who we are?"

Mr. Hamilton kept a straight face. "I have no idea what you're talking about! Now get on out of here, or I'll have to tell your father next time!"

The Kennedy children, still stunned by the discovery, waved goodbye and clambered up the attic steps.

"Can you believe how much we went through today?" Dolley said.

"I know, but I think I know why Dad wanted us to come here. The problem with my friends and our government was getting rough, and I think Dad knew that Mr. Hamilton could answer my questions."

"I think you're right, AJ!" Reagan agreed. "But there's one problem . . ."

They all knew it.

"How do we get back to the Rotunda?" they asked each other.

As if on cue, the American flag portal shone through one of the old doors that lay against the wall.

"Look! It's the void!" Dolley shouted.

"That's it! We all said 'back to the Rotunda'! That must be the cue to get us back!" AJ reasoned.

"Well, c'mon! Dad will be waiting!" Reagan said as the three of them clasped hands once again, jumped, and left all that they had learned about *The Federalist Papers*, Alexander Hamilton, and the portal to history behind them . . .

CHAPTER ELEVEN

"HEY! OW, THAT'S MY ARM!" REAGAN complained when a sneaker stepped on her as the three Kennedy children tumbled out of the doorway and onto the basement floor of the Rotunda.

"Reagan, you're pulling my hair!" Dolley screamed, gripping her hair, which was entangled in Reagan's hands.

"Well, I can't move until AJ gets off of my arm!" she argued.

"My, my! You guys have really got to get a better landing method!" A voice laughed from beside them.

The Kennedys jumped up from their uncomfortable positions on the floor and stood face-to-face with the smiling expressions of their father and Tom.

"Yeah! I guess we better do that, huh?" AJ laughed and pulled his sisters up.

"Did you know all along that we were going to come here?" Dolley asked her father.

"Yes, I did, Miss Dolley." Dad laughed. "I had been thinking about it for a long time and I decided that you were old enough to handle yourselves out there and that Alexander could probably answer AJ's question better than I could. He also happens to be a friend of mine, and I bet that with your red hair and last name, he recognized you as my kids. I can always count on him, you know. He's a good man."

"Wait. So if you know him, and he knows us . . . does that mean . . ." AJ began.

"Yes, sir. When we were boys, Tom and I were best friends, and we always were known for mischief. One day, we found this door, said the right thing at the right time and, well . . . the rest is history."

They all laughed, and Tom added, "That's right! I knew you kids would be smart enough to figure the password out on your own, so I didn't give away the answer. But you certainly did a great job of using your teamwork to get through those boxes! I thought I was going to have to run!"

"Yeah! We thought it seemed strange! That, combined with Dad's weird behavior, threw us off completely!" said Reagan.

Dad laughed. "Well, I'm glad Tom gave you a good chase! And I do hope you enjoyed it, but you can't tell anyone about this. It needs to be a secret. I think you can understand that?" Dad paused as his children nodded. "If someone found out about this . . ."

"They might wanna do it so they can have control of the island?" AJ jumped in.

Dolley and Reagan laughed when Dad and Tom gave blank stares.

"Well, I guess you've learned something we never did!" Tom laughed, and they all joined in until AJ spoke again.

"Well, Dad, I just want to say thank you for that, because I think I found out how to solve the problems for our club," he said.

"And we got to meet Alexander Hamilton!" Reagan added.

"And see how the first Federalist Paper was written and why it was so important to the Constitution being ratified," Dolley chimed in.

"You sure did! And you got to see American history in the making! You even helped *Alexander Hamilton* himself write *The*

Federalist Papers! You're Federalists in the making! Young Federalists, I suppose," Dad said.

AJ laughed. "I love it, Dad!"

"That's what we'll call ourselves!" Reagan added.

Dolley held up the old baseball triumphantly. "To the Young Federalists!"

"To the Young Federalists!" they all shouted.

CHAPTER TWELVE

"SO, AJ, WHAT ARE YOU GOING TO DO WITH your government problems?" Mr. Kennedy asked as the four of them settled into a booth in one of the local cafés right near the Archives.

"Yeah! I found out that there can be such a thing as a good government; we just need to remember that good decisions are the ones that make a fair judgment, and we should really discuss matters together, with everyone's interest in mind," AJ said. "Also, I think that when we first found the money, we all had in mind what we wanted to do with it, and we were doing what Mr. Hamilton told us about. We were all valuing our private interests over what we could do for the club. I think that maybe we could use the money to buy something for our club. That way, all of us can benefit from the money and not just me or any of the other boys."

"I think that's a good plan. Except for one thing . . . I found the owner of that wallet. In fact, as soon as you showed it to me, I knew who it was."

AJ cocked his head. "Who?"

"Mrs. Gloria. She came to me the other day saying she lost it in the park. I told her that we could keep an eye out for the shiny wallet she dropped."

"Oh, well . . ."

"However, when I called her, she did say that she wanted to give you boys a reward." He pulled out one of the ten-dollar bills that they had found in the wallet. "It will be difficult for you to find out what to do with this, but . . ."

"I know just what to do."

"Hey, that's a brilliant idea, AJ!" Jimmy said when AJ told the club the plan and held up the money.

"Yeah, I think it's perfect! We'll use that money to buy a notebook and pen for the new job in our government. That way, we can record all the rules and history of our club!" Tyler said happily. "We can even plan for future projects!"

"I think since AJ was the one who came up with the idea, he should be unanimously elected!" Cole shouted.

"Well, that's it, then!" Mikey said as he clipped an F pin to AJ's shirt.

"Here's to the new Federalist writer!" they all shouted.

AJ smiled and looked down at the ten-dollar bill in his hand.

On the front was a picture of the man who had given him all the answers: Alexander Hamilton. He seemed to be looking at AJ from the past, telling him one more time that when a government looks to the interests of the people, it can be a truly good one.

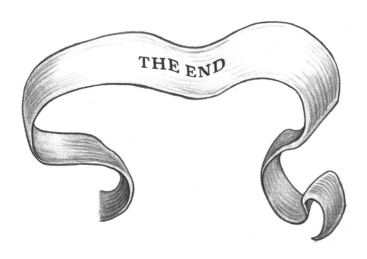

THE END

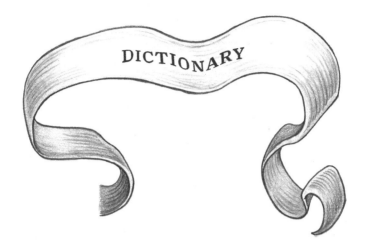

DICTIONARY

REMEMBER THE BOLDED WORDS IN THE story? If you didn't know what they meant or want to learn more about them, read on for a definition!

Abraham Lincoln: Abraham Lincoln was the sixteenth President of the United States. With his famous Emancipation Proclamation and Gettysburg Address, he led the northern states to victory during the Civil War and enacted freedom for enslaved people. He lived from February 12, 1809, to April 15, 1865.

Alexander Hamilton: Alexander Hamilton was the first US Secretary of the Treasury, and there is no doubt that he was one of America's Founding Fathers. He was greatly influential with the people, as can be seen through his writings in *The Federalist Papers*. In addition, he was the founder of the National Bank, a system that loaned the government money so it could help pay off the debts of the states and fund important projects. He lived from January 11, 1755, to July 12, 1804.

Andrew Jackson: President and General Andrew Jackson was a war hero and ferocious fighter in the years before he joined the American government. He served in both branches of Congress and eventually became the seventh President of the United States. He lived from March 15, 1767, to June 8, 1845.

Archivist of the United States: The Archivist of the United States is a historian who is in charge of the treatment and protection of important historical documents which may need special attention because of their age and fragility.

Bill of Rights: The Bill of Rights are the first ten amendments to the Constitution. An amendment is a change or addition to a law, to make it more just for the public good.

Constitution: The Constitution of the United States is the highest law in the American government. It is written in seven articles which detail how the American government should operate.

Declaration of Independence: The Declaration of Independence is a document written by the first United States citizens, declaring their freedom from British rule and their intention to form their own government.

Democratic Republic: This form of government is the type of government that the United States uses; it means that we have some characteristics of a democracy and some of a republic. Our Democratic Republic, as Abraham Lincoln said, is run "of the people, by the people, and for the people!"

Dolley Madison: First Lady Dolley Madison was the wife of President James Madison. She is most famous for her daring choice to save the portrait of George Washington from the burning White House during the War of 1812. She lived from May 20, 1768, to July 12, 1849.

Election: An election is when a group of people voice their opinions by voting for those they want as their representatives.

Eliza Hamilton: Eliza Hamilton was the wife of Alexander Hamilton and a firm advocate of his work. She was also an avid believer in her own works, like becoming the director and co-founder of one of the first orphanages in New York. She lived from August 9, 1757, to November 9, 1854.

Founding Father: A Founding Father is a person who was present at the beginning of an organization or institution—in America's case, the founding of the government.

Government: A government is a body of people who are required to make, execute, and interpret laws for the people. The three parts of the United States government are called the legislative branch (making the laws), the judiciary branch (interpreting the laws), and the executive branch (executing the laws).

House of Representatives (or part of the Legislative branch): The Senate and the House of Representatives make up what we call Congress. The number of representatives for each state depends on the size of the state; as its name suggests, the representatives are meant to represent their state by proposing bills or amendments.

James Madison: James Madison was not only the fourth president of the United States and a Founding Father, but also one of the three writers of *The Federalist Papers*. He lived from March 16, 1751, to June 28, 1836.

John Jay: John Jay was one of the writers of *The Federalist Papers*. He was also the governor of New York and the first chief justice of the Supreme Court. He lived from December 23, 1745, to May 17, 1829.

Liberty: Liberty means that you are free to believe and do as you please, as long as you don't infringe on the liberties of others.

National Archives: The National Archives Museum is in Washington DC, and houses important documents crucial to the meaning and founding of the American government.

Philip, Angelica, and Alexander Hamilton, Jr.: The three children of Alexander and Eliza at the time of the Kennedy childrens' visit. The couple later had James, John, Eliza, and (yes, another) Philip.

President (or the Executive branch): It is the president's job to execute the laws of the government. This means that he or she is responsible for ensuring whichever laws in effect during their administration are followed.

Ratify: To ratify something is to make it legal by collectively agreeing to it.

Ronald Reagan: President Ronald Reagan is most famous for his popularity with the American people and his joyful attitude in representing them. He also encouraged other countries to use their governments wisely and with the people in mind. He lived from February 6, 1911, to June 5, 2004.

Rotunda: The Rotunda is located on the upper floor of the National Archives. It is the round room that displays the Bill of Rights, Constitution, and Declaration of Independence.

Senate (or part of the Legislative branch): The Senate and the House of Representatives make up Congress. Each state gets two senators. Their job is to make sure that the state they represent has all the rights they are entitled to from the Constitution. They also confirm the elections of important officials like the president and Supreme Court justices.

Supreme Court (or the Judiciary branch): In the US government, the Supreme Court is made up of nine justices whose job is to interpret the meaning of the Constitution and decide if the laws of the government are aligned with the Constitution.

The Federalist Papers: A series of eighty-five papers written to the people of New York promoting the ratification of the Constitution. They were written between 1787 and 1788.

Theodore Roosevelt: Theodore Roosevelt was a very thoughtful man and the twenty-sixth president of the United States. He was a great supporter of the environment and of natural resources; he promoted the growth of national parks and conservation areas. He lived from October 27, 1858, to January 6, 1919.

Vote: A vote is an opinion someone expresses during an election.

ALEXANDER HAMILTON'S FIRST FEDERALIST Paper came out at the end of 1787 (and with the help of some friends). It was very successful and popular with the New York crowd. Don't worry if you're not able to understand it just yet; this is a copy for your own private use when, one day, you will be able to understand it.

Also, all three writers at first signed their name "Publius" to hide their identities, but after a while, word got out that it was Hamilton, Jay, and Madison who wrote the papers.

Presenting Hamilton's First Paper . . .

To the People of the State of New York:

AFTER an unequivocal experience of the inefficiency of the subsisting federal government, you are called upon to deliberate on a new Constitution for the United States of America. The subject speaks its own importance; comprehending in its consequences nothing less than the existence of the union, the safety and welfare of the parts of which it is composed, the fate of an empire in many respects the most interesting in the world. It has been frequently remarked that it seems to have been reserved to the people of this country, by their conduct and example, to decide the important question, whether societies of men are really capable or not of establishing good government from reflection and choice, or whether they are forever destined to depend for their political constitutions on accident and force. If there be any truth in the remark, the crisis at which we are arrived may with propriety be regarded as the era in which that decision is to be made; and a wrong election of the part we shall act may, in this view, deserve to be considered as the general misfortune of mankind.

This idea will add the inducements of philanthropy to those of patriotism, to heighten the solicitude which all considerate and good men must feel for the event. Happy will it be if our choice should be directed by a judicious estimate of our true interests, unperplexed and unbiased by considerations not connected with the public good. But this is a thing more ardently to be wished than seriously to be expected. The plan offered to our deliberations affects too many particular interests, innovates upon too many local institutions, not to involve in its discussion a variety of objects foreign to its merits, and of views, passions and prejudices little favorable to the discovery of truth.

Among the most formidable of the obstacles which the new Constitution will have to encounter may readily be distinguished the obvious interest of a certain class of men in every State to resist all changes which may hazard a diminution of the power, emolument, and consequence of the offices they hold under the State establishments; and the perverted ambition of another class of men, who will either hope to aggrandize themselves by the confusions of their country, or will flatter themselves with fairer prospects of elevation from the subdivision of the empire into several partial confederacies than from its union under one government.

It is not, however, my design to dwell upon observations of this nature. I am well aware that it would be disingenuous to resolve indiscriminately the opposition of any set of men (merely because their situations might subject them to suspicion) into interested or ambitious views. Candor will oblige us to admit that even such men may be actuated by upright intentions; and it cannot be doubted that much of the opposition which has made its appearance, or may hereafter make its appearance, will spring from sources, blameless at least, if not respectable—the honest errors of minds led astray by preconceived jealousies and fears. So numerous indeed and so powerful are the causes which serve to give a false bias to the judgment, that we, upon many occasions, see wise and good men on the wrong as well as on the right side of questions of the first magnitude to society. This circumstance, if duly attended to, would furnish a lesson of moderation to those who are ever so much persuaded of their being in the right in any controversy. And a further reason for caution, in this respect, might be drawn from the reflection that we are not always sure that those who advocate the truth are influenced by purer principles than their antagonists. Ambition, avarice, personal animosity, party opposition, and many other motives not more laudable than these, are apt to operate as well upon those who support as those who oppose the right side of a question. Were there not even these inducements to moderation, nothing could be more ill-judged than that intolerant spirit which has, at all times, characterized political parties. For in politics, as in religion, it is equally absurd to aim at making proselytes by fire and sword. Heresies in either can rarely be cured by persecution.

And yet, however just these sentiments will be allowed to be, we have already sufficient indications that it will happen in this as in all former cases of great national discussion. A torrent of angry and malignant passions will be let loose. To judge from the conduct of the opposite parties, we shall be led to conclude that they will mutually hope to evince the justness of their opinions, and to increase the number of their converts by the loudness of their declamations and the bitterness of their invectives. An enlightened zeal for the energy and efficiency of government will be stigmatized as the offspring of a temper fond of despotic power and hostile to the principles of liberty. An over-scrupulous jealousy of danger to the rights of the people, which is more commonly the fault of the head than of the heart, will be represented as mere pretense and artifice, the stale bait for popularity at the expense of the public good. It will be forgotten, on the one hand, that jealousy is the usual concomitant of love, and that the noble enthusiasm of liberty is apt to be infected with a spirit of narrow and illiberal distrust. On the other hand, it will be equally forgotten that the vigor of government is essential to the security of liberty; that, in the contemplation of a sound and well-informed judgment, their interest can never be separated; and that a dangerous ambition more often lurks behind the specious mask of zeal for the rights of the people than under the forbidden appearance of zeal for the firmness and efficiency of government. History will teach us that the former has been found a much more certain road to the introduction of despotism than the latter, and that of those men who have overturned the liberties of republics, the greatest number have begun their career by paying an obsequious court to the people; commencing demagogues, and ending tyrants.

In the course of the preceding observations, I have had an eye, my fellow-citizens, to putting you upon your guard against all attempts, from whatever quarter, to influence your decision in a matter of the utmost moment to your welfare, by any impressions other than those which may result from the evidence of truth. You will, no doubt, at the same time, have collected from the general scope of them, that they proceed from a source not unfriendly to the new Constitution. Yes, my countrymen, I own to you that, after having given it an attentive consideration, I am clearly of opinion it is your interest to adopt it. I am convinced that this is the safest course for your liberty, your dignity, and your happiness. I affect not reserves which I do not feel. I will not amuse you with an appearance of deliberation when I have decided. I frankly acknowledge to you my convictions, and I will freely lay before you the reasons on which they are founded. The consciousness of good intentions disdains ambiguity. I shall not, however, multiply professions on this head. My motives must remain in the depository of my own breast. My arguments will be open to all, and may be judged of by all. They shall at least be offered in a spirit which will not disgrace the cause of truth.

I propose, in a series of papers, to discuss the following interesting particulars: The utility of the union to your political prosperity, the insufficiency of the present confederation to preserve that union, the necessity of a government at least equally energetic with the one proposed, to the attainment of this object, the conformity of the proposed constitution to the true principles of republican government, its analogy to your own state constitution and lastly, the additional security which its adoption will afford to the preservation of that species of government, to liberty, and to property.

In the progress of this discussion I shall endeavor to give a satisfactory answer to all the objections which shall have made their appearance, that may seem to have any claim to your attention.

It may perhaps be thought superfluous to offer arguments to prove the utility of the UNION, a point, no doubt, deeply engraved on the hearts of the great body of the people in every State, and one, which it may be imagined, has no adversaries. But the fact is, that we already hear it whispered in the private circles of those who oppose the new Constitution, that the thirteen States are of too great extent for any general system, and that we must of necessity resort to separate confederacies of distinct portions of the whole. This doctrine will, in all probability, be gradually propagated, till it has votaries enough to countenance an open avowal of it. For nothing can be more evident, to those who are able to take an enlarged view of the subject, than the alternative of an adoption of the new Constitution or a dismemberment of the Union. It will therefore be of use to begin by examining the advantages of that Union, the certain evils, and the probable dangers, to which every State will be exposed from its dissolution. This shall accordingly constitute the subject of my next address.

Publius.

ABIGAIL READLINGER IS A CURRENT high school junior at The Wilberforce School, located in Princeton, New Jersey, where she enjoys participating year-round on both the sport and debating teams. Homebound during the pandemic, Abigail was inspired to create her first draft of *The Young Federalists*. Almost two years later, she is thrilled to have her whim become a reality and hopes readers will enjoy the lives of Reagan, AJ, and Dolley as much as she enjoyed creating them. In her free time, Abigail enjoys horseback riding, creative writing, and rereading all of her favorite Agatha Christie novels. She has two younger siblings named Sarah and Doc, as well as an honorary third sibling—her yellow lab, Daisy.